Published by
Delacorte Press
Bantam Doubleday Dell Publishing Group, Inc.
666 Fifth Avenue
New York, New York 10103
This work was first published in Great Britain in 1990
by Hamish Hamilton Ltd. as MRS CHRISTMAS.
Copyright © 1990 by Penny Ives
The trademark Delacorte Press® is registered in the
U.S. Patent and Trademark Office.

Library of Congress Cataloging in Publication Data
Ives, Penny.
Mrs. Santa Claus / Penny Ives.
p.   cm.
Summary: Santa's resourceful wife delivers the presents on Christmas Eve
when he and the reindeer become ill.
ISBN 0-385-30302-5. — ISBN 0-385-30303-3 (lib. bdg.)
[1. Santa Claus — Fiction. 2. Christmas — Fiction. 3. Sex role — Fiction.]
I. Title.
PZ7.I949Mr1991   [E] — dc20   90-49468   CIP   AC

Manufactured in England

November 1991

10   9   8   7   6   5   4   3   2   1

Mrs. Santa Claus

Penny Ives

DELACORTE PRESS • NEW YORK

Last Christmas there was a near calamity. One morning in late December, Santa Claus woke up and found that he felt quite ill.

"Just look at you!" cried Mrs. Santa Claus. "You're all covered in spots. How ever will I finish making all these presents by myself?"

"I'd better hurry up and feed the reindeer," Mrs. Santa Claus said to herself.

But when she went into the stable she could hardly believe her eyes. The *reindeer* were covered in spots too! She decided to give them a dose of medicine while she considered what to do next.

First she put on her winter coat and went outside with her pet birds. Hundreds of letters to Santa Claus had fallen with the snow during the night. Together they gathered them all up.

Mrs. Santa Claus read every letter. Then she rolled up her sleeves. Still so many toys to finish, even though she and Santa Claus had been working hard all year—ever since last Christmas in fact!

All day Mrs. Santa Claus sewed and sewed and glued until everything was done.

But then she had a worrying thought. Without the reindeer how would she deliver the toys?

Whoopee! She suddenly had a brilliant idea. She would turn her bicycle into a flying machine!

The vacuum cleaner would power her takeoff! She searched high and low in the cupboard for everything else that she needed.

She fixed the vacuum so that it would blow air out instead of sucking it in.

Carefully she linked the pedals to the motor. The faster she pedaled, the faster it would go.

At last! The flying machine was ready! Mrs. Santa Claus felt very pleased with herself!

Mrs. Santa Claus labeled each of the presents and stowed them away in her basket. One or two were rather large and proved to be quite troublesome!

Finally she put on her red suit and hat. No one would recognize her now!

Outside it was very cold. Mrs. Santa Claus cleared a
small runway in the snow ready for takeoff.

Mrs. Claus's goose and chicken flapped their wings
hard and she pedaled furiously.

Round and round and round spun the wheels until the
machine lifted silently into the air.

Mrs. Santa Claus was flying!

Further and further flew Mrs. Santa Claus until she saw a small town. She guided the bicycle in to land on a snowy rooftop.

Tying a long rope around the chimney, she lowered herself down.

There! She had soot all over her lovely red suit. How did Santa Claus seem to keep so clean?

Mrs. Santa Claus went up and down chimneys all night until the very last present had been delivered and her baskets were empty. Now she must make the journey home.

It seemed such a very long way. Suddenly
Mrs. Santa Claus spotted a faint glow of lights.

It was Santa Claus and the reindeer guiding her
in to land!

They must be better! All their spots had gone! "I'm so glad you're home safely," said Santa Claus. "Come and sit down, dear, and take your boots off. I'll go and run you a lovely hot bath."

Mrs. Santa Claus enjoyed a long, hot soak. When she felt better she went downstairs, where there was a wonderful surprise waiting for her...

Santa Claus had made a special breakfast with presents for everyone!

Merry Christmas!